W9-BID-445

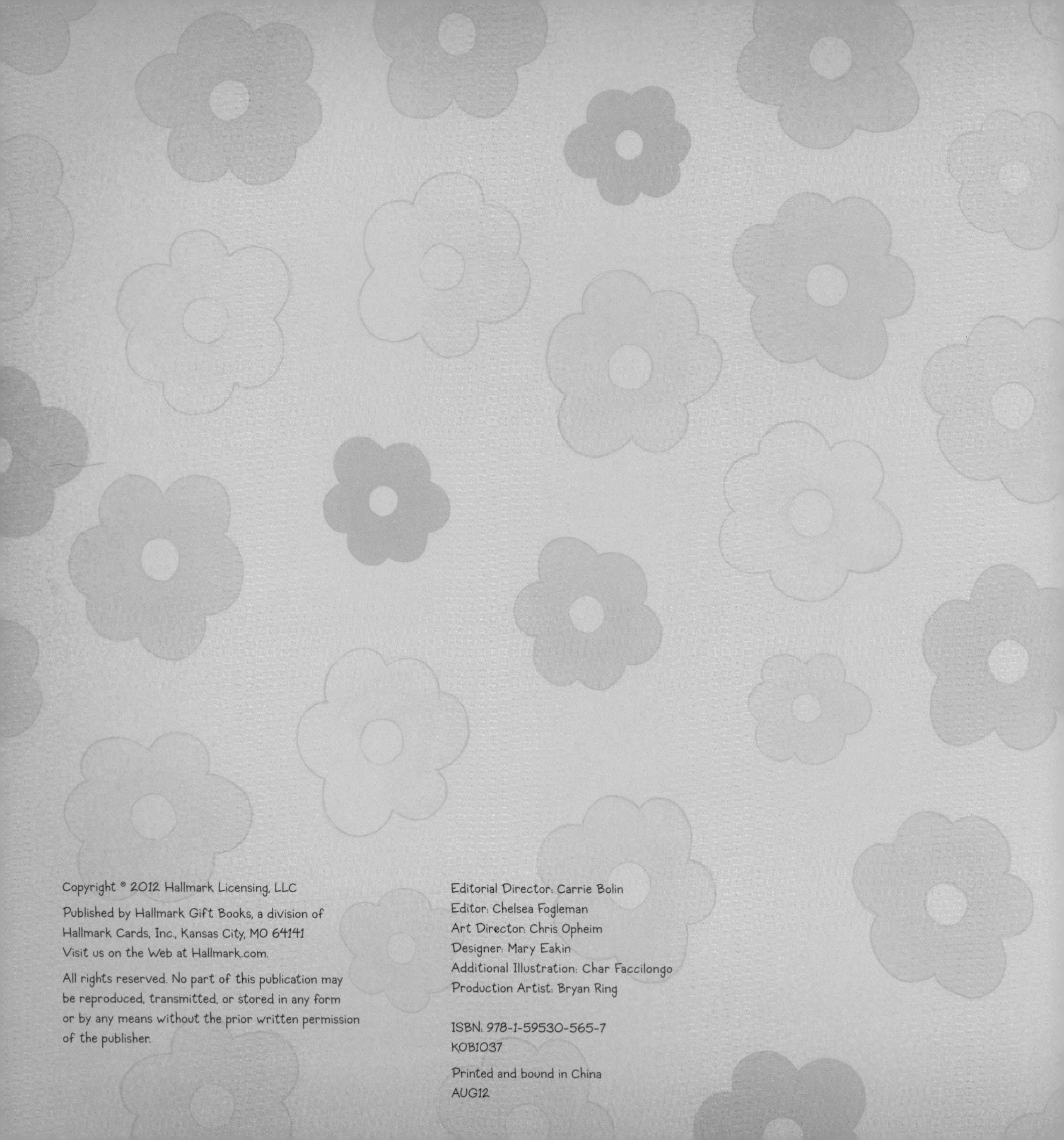

Copyright © 2012 Hallmark Licensing, LLC

Published by Hallmark Gift Books, a division of
Hallmark Cards, Inc., Kansas City, MO 64141
Visit us on the Web at Hallmark.com.

All rights reserved. No part of this publication may
be reproduced, transmitted, or stored in any form
or by any means without the prior written permission
of the publisher.

Editorial Director: Carrie Bolin
Editor: Chelsea Fogleman
Art Director: Chris Opheim
Designer: Mary Eakin
Additional Illustration: Char Faccilongo
Production Artist: Bryan Ring

ISBN: 978-1-59530-565-7
KOB1037

Printed and bound in China
AUG12

A Gift For

From

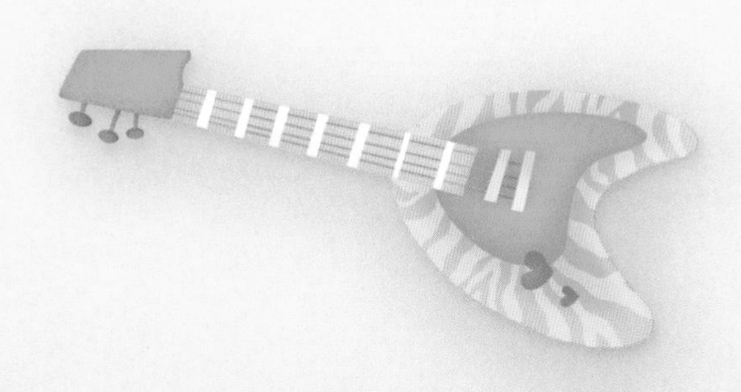

How to Use Your Interactive Story Buddy™

1. Activate your Story Buddy™ by pressing the "On / Off" button on the ear.
2. Read the story aloud in a quiet place. Speak in a clear voice when you see the highlighted phrases.
3. Listen to your Story Buddy™ respond with several different phrases throughout the book.

Clarity and speed of reading affect the way Posey™ responds. She may not always respond to young children.

Watch for even more Interactive Story Buddy™ characters. For more information, visit us on the Web at Hallmark.com/StoryBuddy.

Hallmark's **I Reply Technology** brings your Story Buddy™ to life! When you read the key phrases out loud, your Story Buddy™ gives a variety of responses, so each time you read feels as magical as the first.

BOOK 3

Posey and the Purrfect Song

By Katherine Stano
Illustrated by Maria Sarria

Hallmark gift books

There were many places Posey liked, but she especially liked her bedroom. It was the only room in her house with green carpet. It reminded her of a grassy meadow. Sometimes she pretended she was twirling through the French countryside. She'd flop on the pretend grass and say, "My room is positively loads of fun!"

One morning, Posey woke up in her bedroom. A catchy new song was playing on her clock radio.

Posey sang the song while brushing her fur. She whistled it while tying her shoes. She hummed it while eating a tuna sandwich.

"It's a PURRfect day!

Meow! Meow! Meow!"

Soon enough, the song got old. Posey tried really hard to forget the tune. She sang another song. She disco-danced. She put her paws to her ears and chanted, "LA LA LA!"

Finally, it worked. No more song! Posey sipped a milkshake to celebrate. "Hip hip hooray!"

LA
La
LA
la
La
la
LA
LA

Then, while Posey sat at the kitchen table, her brother, Cub, ran into the room.

He sang out like a rock star. "It's a PURRfect day! Meow! Meow! Meow!"

Posey gritted her teeth. "NO! NO! NO!"

But it was too late—the song was back. Poor Posey! This was very bad news.

Luckily, Posey's friends were coming over to play. "I'll have fun playing with Fluff, Kit, and Tabby. They'll help me forget that song." She looked out the window to see if anyone was there yet.

Cub asked, "Will your friends want to see my pet frogs?"

"Maybe," she answered, even though she wasn't exactly listening. Waiting for her friends, Posey was seriously excited.

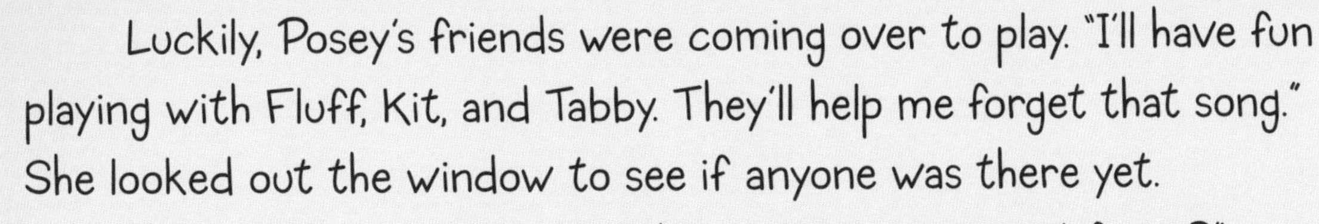

When Posey's friends arrived, they all sang the song together. Kit sounded like a pop diva. Fluff added harmony. And Tabby sang with heart and soul, even though she was a little off-key (okay, a LOT off-key).

With her friends there, Posey almost liked the song. "I know what we should do," she said. "Let's start a band."

Everyone clapped. A band—what a marvelous idea!

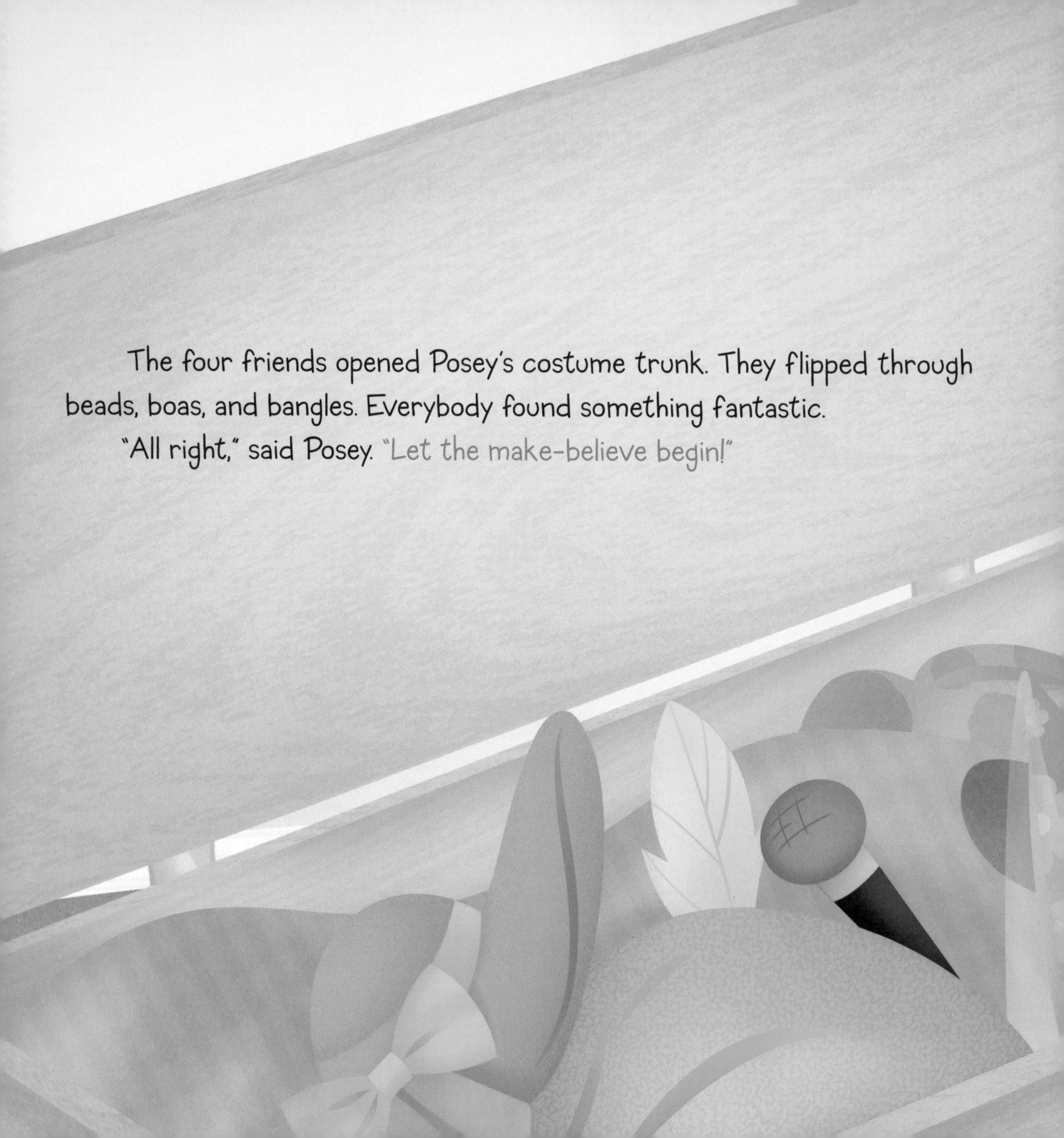

The four friends opened Posey's costume trunk. They flipped through beads, boas, and bangles. Everybody found something fantastic.

"All right," said Posey. "Let the make-believe begin!"

They walked into the living room singing their song. "It's a PURRfect day! Meow! Meow! Meow!" Tabby hit a high note and threw back her arms.

That was when it happened. Tabby accidentally knocked over the frog cage.

Posey gasped, looking out the open window. "The frogs are gone!" Everyone gulped. This was very bad news.

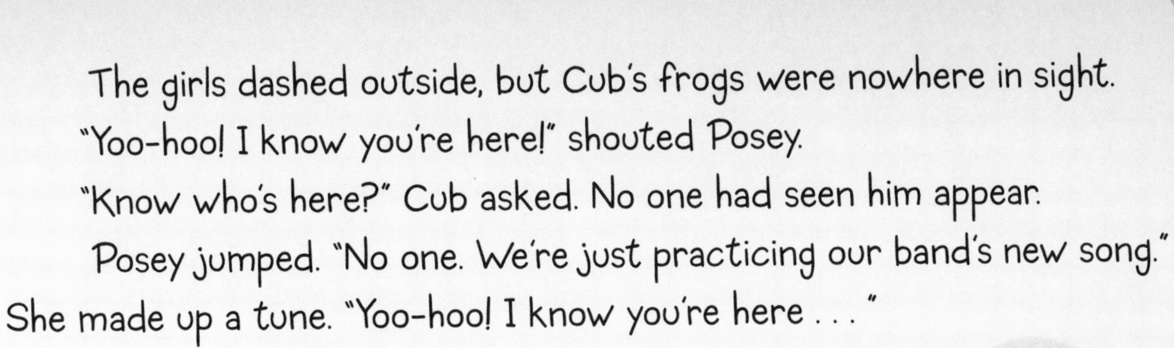

The girls dashed outside, but Cub's frogs were nowhere in sight.

"Yoo-hoo! I know you're here!" shouted Posey.

"Know who's here?" Cub asked. No one had seen him appear.

Posey jumped. "No one. We're just practicing our band's new song." She made up a tune. "Yoo-hoo! I know you're here . . . "

Suddenly, a frog jumped from a flower bed and over Posey's head. "I see you!" she cried. She reached for the frog but instead slipped and fell.

The other girls had the same bad luck. They were falling all over the place and getting stuck in the mud. They had grass stains everywhere.

Posey just couldn't believe it.

Cub laughed as he watched the girls and frogs hop everywhere. At last, he whistled sharply. Instantly, the frogs turned and hopped toward him.

He patted their heads.

The girls looked on, shocked. "You could do that the WHOLE time?" Posey grumbled.

Cub smiled. "What? I'm a frog trainer."

At last, Posey and her pals looked down at their ruined clothes.
"Yuck! We're all dirty!" said Fluff.
"This is SO not cool," said Tabby.

Posey wiped mud off her whiskers. Their rock star afternoon was a complete disaster. What was a girl to do?

"Well," said Posey, "we can't play rock stars anymore. That means there's only one thing to do . . . we'll have to play Jungle Explorers!"

Everyone's faces brightened. "Yeah! Yeah!" the others cried.

It really was a purrfect day. Posey smiled and thought, "You can always have fun if you have a great imagination!"

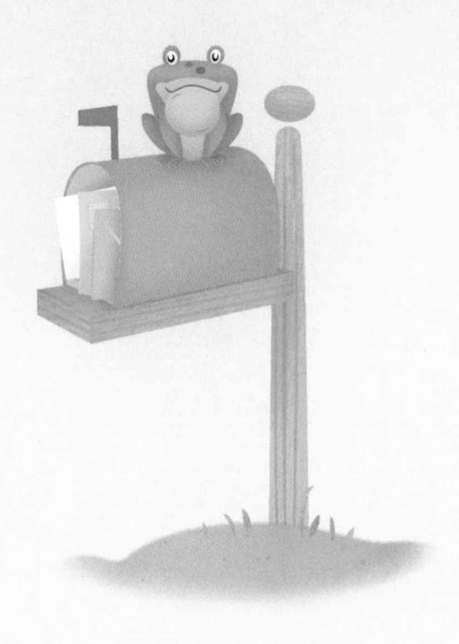

Did you have fun with Posey™?
We would love to hear from you!

Please send your comments to:
Hallmark Book Feedback
P.O. Box 419034
Mail Drop 215
Kansas City, MO 64141

Or e-mail us at:
booknotes@hallmark.com